ANTIPENSIONISTIC VIRUS

BY FIORDELISI LUIGI

(English edition)

AUTHOR

Eng.Fiordelisi Luigi, born in Naples on 10-01-1950 master's degree in engineering electronic , computers and automatic controls. After several years of work at   companies in the strategic sector (Montedison, Selenia, etc. .) as a Designer, he started working as an technical industrial IT teacher and periodic consultant both in Italy and abroad (Cairo, Nigeria) for the Eni group. He conceived and patented, created the "Computerized shopping trolley .." presented live by Rai Uno "I Cervelloni". Among the artistic experiences it is worth mentioning that as a student he worked as an appearance in the film "Excellent cadavers" with Lino Ventura. Directed by Franco Rosi.

Introduction

*The book deals with the problem of retirees through the story dr Tkinking   (**Italian** dr Pensi= man thinking " ,,,) new aspirant, assisted by dr Suppository (**Italian** dr Supposti = man receiving suppository ...) the next aspirant and mr Misfortune (**Italian** signore Sventura = unfortunate man...) , fresh retiree. The tone is ironic, but covered by a veiled tragedy. When it was his turn, the government declared that there was no money, too many retirees. Hence a general* *protest, which put the government in crisis. That new beginning was a favorable policy: pension increase, etc. This sound strange, so much so that the statistics revealed a sharp increase in mortality for pensioners. Was it pure coincidence or was there a link with the new pension policy? So dr Thinking and dr Suppository turned into detectives and discovered a diabolical plan to eliminate pensioners with "anti-tension" viruses, and that ... From   series of ironic vicissitudes, in search of an antidote, also to save the fresh friend ... "retired". Can overcome his .. adventure? Will they manage to foil the government 's plan ? But above all dr Thinking will become a ....dr Thinking ... honoured ?*

Acknowledgments

To women more care: it was teacher . Maria Acunzo for encouragement, deep esteem and years of teaching together, Luisamaria, Marg, Tonia who with their problems is the least monotonous life!

INDEX

CHAPTER I

THE CRISIS OF THE PENSION SYSTEM

At seven, the daily sound of the alarm clock dissolved dr. Thinking Igino, primary - for over thirty years - of the "Fatebenefratelli " hospital in Rome: now he was missing the retreat: another year and in the end his stressful lifestyle would end. He leaned lazily to silence the alarm clock and stayed in bed for a while longer. dr Thinking , specialized in virology and clinical immunology, had become an excellent doctor more by his father's will than by his own vocation. Instead, his love of fine arts and literature was congenial to him and he was particularly fascinated by it. It is therefore easy to understand how much a simple pensioner wished to be dedicated to these passions. He was cheerful and cunning in his daily life, depending on how he presented himself, without forgetting to grasp his aspects. His wife – mrs Break Ermenziana (breaking boxes...)- got up and, as usual, made good coffee and offered it to him urging him to get up. The Igino, while tasting his coffee with taste, thought: "I can't wait for it to end, I can't take it anymore. What bad luck is mine! ... Fortunately this year I will retire and finally I can also sleep as much I want. "He got up, got ready, said goodbye to Ermenziana and left; his wife, punctual as always, slipped again under the covers to laze. dr Thinking, arrived at the newsstand, bought his favorite newspaper with the hope of reading good news, but - alas! - the first thing he happened to read was: ... the government does not guarantee the payment of pensions ... "What a greeting!" .... I think. The news was colder than a cold shower; unfortunately, however, the indifferent time has passed and dr. Thinking - more thoughtful than usual - he hurried to go to work, to the " Fatebenefratelli " hospital. After the usual small stop at the bar, at the hospital entrance, to sip another coffee, together with his friend and colleague dr Suppository an expert in pharmacology, thought of starting his working day. But ... dr Suppository stopped him asking him: "Did you know the news about pensions, do you think?" "I saw the first page, but I have not read the article yet" "The government can no longer guarantee the payment of pensions, why not there is more money! " dr Suppository added. "And it seemed to you, right now that it's up to us! These children of ...! Let me see." They leafed through the newspaper and read the article. So, dr Thinking , ironically began the comment aloud: ... the government declares the crisis of the social security system; for its reform various hypotheses began to emerge: the deputy Hon. Holiday (= Vacanza)   proposes the stop in service up to eighty years; someone proposes a kind of incentive to stay up to a hundred years, so that later - if God wants - he can enjoy life with a more adequate pension! And this always in the interest of the citizen! ... dr Suppository - similar to those who are immersed in meditation suddenly continue to think out loud - he commented "   "After so many years of contributions and waiting! ... but, couldn't they tell us before taking service?" dr Thinking, laughing nervously, replied: "Yes, so no one would have gone to work! and Supposedly - almost without realizing dr Thinking 's intervention - he continued:" You want to see that we will also have to collect the money to pay government debts ? But, - why don't they cut parliamentarians' pensions? Why don't they reduce waste? They want to save on poor retirees ... We will see! Until I am sure that I will receive the pension, I will not abandon my job. "At this point the sense of duty forced them to stop the conversation and to dedicate themselves, as always with conscience, each to their own work. Of course, pensions were on the agenda and the comments of   dr

Thinking and dr Suppository were more or less similar among all the workers, and not only among those of the " Fatebenefratelli " hospital . In fact, when dr Thinking came to his department, a colleague asked him if he was aware of the latest news on pensions, and yet another. "Did you know they want to save on pensions?" and yet another: "Only now do they realize they have no money ?!" The dr. Thinking of each one in response: "Yes, yes, but it hasn't been said yet" or "Yes, yes, don't remind me!" He was now intent on his work, when a unionist colleague also came to his department to inform everyone. "Tomorrow, there is a national strike to protest the government's bad intentions about pensions. There will be a procession to Piazza del Popolo (square..). You are all invited to participate ". Dr Thinking had always been a quiet man, diligent in his work and had never been interested in union problems, but this time he was too upset to give up a chance to explode, and said: "I'll be there too and in the front row not only that, but I will also encourage others to take part in it ". In truth there was nothing to convince, because all the workers were indistinctly on a war footing. In fact, the discussions and debates continued for the whole day, and not only in the

"Fatebenefratelli " hospital. At the end of his working day, dr. Thinking came home, he turned on the television to hear the news: "... there is no money, we need to reform the pension system, maybe to extend the retirement age, therefore, the stay in service as much as possible" Oh ! it looks like they were waiting for me! I did not know that my pension was such as to contribute to the savings of the state! "So saying, he went to sleep, but the nightmares, the agitation tormented him no less than the phone call of his friend Suppositories." Hello, dr Thinking, sorry time. It's three o'clock but it's that I can't sleep. "" Whoever you say it, it's up to me to get up early in the morning for who knows how long   more! "" You have to go down to the square, "dr Suppository replied," even if we never did. " "I agree with you! But keep calm, if God wants, and if we know how to deserve it, it will help us solve our problem. But ...,dr Suppository , what can we do ?! Do you want to die ahead of time for sorrow ? "" Of course not! "" Then let's sleep. See you tomorrow ... "They hung up. During the night, dr. Thinking _ dreamed of filling out the pension application, then of being in the competent office. Here the employee said to him: "Dr. Thinking , it is not yet your time, I will go back

further, maybe in ten years, or rather, I am sorry, according to the new circular, in a hundred years". He woke up with a start, drenched in sweat, bleached in the face and stammering ... one hundred,, one hundred,. one hundred, ..to years !. When he woke up completely, realizing the reality he said: "A hundred years in jail I would give them to that bunch of morons; even for the night I am not at ease! There is little to do, the strength of the state is time: lives longer than any citizen and does   not pay! "So saying, he fell asleep again, despite so many nightmares .When the alarm rang on time at seven, he was already awake, shaved and dressed, ready to do battle: "Come back in a hundred years ..." "Alli mortacci sua" (in Roman " to his   dead...)   was repeating to himself. The alarm went on, but he, taken by these thoughts, did not bother to silence it. Ms Rompi (=ms Breaking boxes..) woke up and almost screamed in anger: "Wake up Igino, stop that damned alarm clock!" Rompi hadn't even bothered to get up to make coffee. Furthermore, comfortably lying on the bed, and without ever having had work experience, she incited the already tormented husband not to be late for work. This time the Igino went away without even saying goodbye! When he arrived at the hospital bar he met dr Suppository who together with other workers, was already ready for the demonstration. There were many banners: "Government do not delude you, we will force you to pay pensions "" We will know how to give up everything but not our rights ". "If necessary, we will hibernate but we will not lose the pension" etc. Thus began the great demonstration, which was attended by workers from all parts of Italy. Later there were others, until the crisis of the Government was made known. Not much time passed and dr. Thinking one day learned from your newspaper that the new government not only ensured the rights already acquired for pensions, but even provided short and long-term economic improvements ... "Finally, here we are - hurray! - he exclaimed - I hope, however , that is not a bluff. So saying, he went immediately to the hospital bar where he found everyone in the party: "You saw, we did it" exclaimed the unionist friend. "You were right," replied dr Thinking and in a impetus for joy, she embraced him as a sign of gratitude and esteem. Then, raising a glass, addressing those present he added: "I propose a toast:" Retired friends present and future, to the new ruling class life and well-being; they knew how to understand our needs and our rights; they wanted and knew prepare a serene, peaceful old age, after a long and tiring work life. Our recognition and applause go to them. ""Hurray! "Exclaimed all those present. Many of them had known each other and had fraternized on the occasion of the protest. Only one problem had united them: retirement. In the days that followed, serenity returned to the various workplaces, so dr Thinking began to live happily in anticipation of the big day, when he would submit his pension application.

CHAPTER II

REFORM AND INSTITUTION OF THE NEW NATIONAL PENSION FUND, WITH ASTERISK (F.N.P.N. *)

The dr. Thinking that day stopped at the usual bar, and for coffee and for any news: "The government is reforming the social security system ..." they said: "No fear for pensioners, because and unused salary levels touched. .. "and so on. It seems to me that the lesson is useful", a comment from dr Thinking , and dr Suppository added: "Yes, after our protest, it seems so." "You always have to react, to get something," commented a present. They all seemed satisfied! Time passed and a new ghost began to take shape: the financial sector! The political situation begins to be always confused, as well as the economic one. It is not possible to make ends meet, since outgoing expenses, especially those for paying pensions, cannot be touched. One fine day we heard of the appointment of the new budget minister; a few days later, there was talk of "government of the technicians"! Since then, there have been new political elections. Naturally, a new government was formed which, among other things, undertook to implement a reform of the social security system *such as to reduce waste and improve the retirement level of retirees. By now it seemed done. After a few days, dr. Think turning on the TV, hear: "The social security system has been reformed, and the" New national pension fund, indicated with the abbreviation F.N.P.N. * has been established * Dr. Furbetti, assisted by a committee of experts. The new and prudent management, upon declaration of the new president, will be able - in a short time - to significantly increase the pension allowance. "" Then it is really done, by now, at least so it seems to me! "Commented _ dr Thinking and decided to inform your friend dr Suppository by phone. "You heard on television, now we can finally retire, and there will also be increases." "I am really happy," replied Suppository, "since yours is approaching and then my turn. Tomorrow we meet at the "Buontempone" restaurant for a dinner. Also warn mr Misfortune, who - poor low - has just retired. So they greeted each other happier than was a friend of theirs and had worked as a nurses at the same hospital for many years, until he retired, coincidentally, just the previous week. Dr Thinking phoned him and informed him of possible increases he concluded: "Other than mr Misfortune, you are just lucky! "... And mr Misfortune ... he was happy! The next*

*day, after leaving work, they all met in the restaurant"
Buontempone ", as agreed." Finally a little serenity –
exclaimed dr. Suppository - it looks really done! "You think
he commented:" Indeed, not only can we retire, but for the
first time in the history of retirement there is talk of
increases. This new F.N.P.N. * fund seems organized and
managed by a certain dr Sly (Italian dr. Furbetti), who, it
seems, is really smart. Of course the surname dr Slyi serves
to make the idea! One thing, however, continually comes
back to me: what does that asterisk mean after the initials
FNPN? "" It seems that the committee of expert collaborators
of the president is made up of men of great value, "added
Suppositories." Of course, to talk about the increase. But ...
when did such a thing ever happen? "Echoed dr Thinking
and mr Misfortune. At this point dr Thinking stood up and
raising a glass full of wine, said:" Gentlemen, let's drink to
the health of dr Sly (Italian dr. Furbetti)i, new president, so
that he doesn't do it ... Also I invite you all to dinner here, as
soon as I retire! "So saying, they toasted. With great
euphoria they spent the whole evening, between one dish and
another very well accompanied from sparkling glasses full of
doc wine dr Thinking did not want to miss the opportunity*

to show off his culture, and to teach friends the art of drinking, he recited a poetic composition, chosen from the XIII century goliardic poetry: " *Bibe primum (latin language)*

bibe totum

et secundum usque ad fundum,

bibe tertium sicut primum

sic placet bibere inum. "

translated means :

"Drink the first one,

drink it all

and the second all the way drink the third as the first

so he likes to drink wine. "

In the end, everyone applauded for a long time and, brisk and euphoric, said goodbye. In the following days the mass media gave great importance especially to the results obtained in the dr Thinking on sector. There were many praises for both the new government and the budget minister, and in particular for the fund's new president, dr. Sly (Italian dr Furbetti) .The results obtained, in the current opinion, were deservedly attributed to the new party that led the ruling coalition. In fact, the pension was close to all citizens, and the good news about it produced an increase in consensus and sympathy for the majority party. This also did them good hope for a big victory in the upcoming political elections.

CHAPTER III

INCREASE IN THE RETIREMENT MORTALITY INDEX

After a few months, everything seemed normalized.One day the dr Sly (Italian dr. Furbetti) on television announced: "Finally, as scheduled, the accounts have been cleared. We will soon be able to increase the pension allowance at all levels, which - as is well known - has never happened in the history of pensions. Best wishes to all pensioners! " When dr Thinking met friends at the hospital bar, they congratulated him: "One more month, dear dr Thinking , and you go on vacation for life too!" they said to him. He replied: "Do not be a jeweler: wheat is safe only when it is in the barrel! -And in saying this he made a ... grenadine-. Celebrate also dr Suppository that he will retire immediately after me!". These were the recurring comments, when one day, leafing through the daily newspaper, dr. _Thinking was struck by a piece of news: "The statistics institute has noticed an increase in the mortality index for some months, particularly accentuated - especially among pensioners - in the very last few times. He immediately informed his friends:" You want to see now that everything is in order, it takes fate! "Commented mr

*Misfortune." We hope not, " dr Suppository added. And you think:" Of course it's a strange fact! "" What ?! "asked the other two anxiously "It is strange that people die two months after retiring. At most they manage to collect one or two pensions. "But ... to that country! "mr Misfortune replied, and went away all intent on anti-icing rites. "What do you think?" dr Suppository asked dr. Thinklng. "I confess that all this worries me, it would be appropriate to deepen before retiring. dr Thinking about it, these increases are not normal: here cat breeds! It has always been said that retirees weigh heavily on the budget, which are unproductive .... and now an increase! " "It's true," dr Suppository replied and added: "and then this V.A.P. * vaccine to retire, I wonder what it is for! How much care!" ... It should be known that, among the certificates to be attached for retirement, there was the declaration that they had been subjected to the "going into retirement" vaccine, known with the abbreviation V.A.P. *, practiced at any health unit. It had been developed to protect citizens from possible infections reported in the various work environments. This is in the interest of all citizens, as was said around. The dr. Thinking he said: "I really don't like this story, dr Suppository, we need to* *investigate. Forget about mr Misfortune, it is no longer ours, and if we find out something   serious, it is better that I don't know it right away. Unfortunately it will soon be up to me and then to you, retire. " "Yes, you are right, but what do you propose to do?"   "Let's pay a visit to the offices of the F.N.P.N. * body and try to discover something in the archives" replied dr Thinking   "But how do you do it?" .. replied dr Suppository. "Do not worry". They met for the next day, in the evening, right in front of the new institution, at the corner of the bar "Il conspirato". Then they said goodbye.*

CHAPTER IV

DISCOVERY OF THE PENSION PAYMENT CANCELLATION PLAN (P.A.P.P.)

The next day, dr Thinking and dr Suppository met at the "Il conspirator " bar as agreed. Posing as inspectors, they managed to deceive the surveillance service and access the offices of the new pension institution. As soon as they entered, they started looking for any useful information to understand whether the death of the pensioners was pure coincidence or hid some diabolical plan. They searched everywhere: drawers, shelves, ... until dr Thinking, convinced of having to search the computer archives, urged his friend to turn on the computer network, since he was the only one able to do it. Dr Suppository set to work immediately and together the two doctors began a stressful search in the various computer archives. This search lasted until almost dawn. Suddenly, while the search seemed unsuccessful, a video appeared on the video: "Enter the secret code, if you want to read in this archive!" "What the hell is this code?" dr Suppository wondered. "I need a secret word, yes in short a word known only by those who can access the archive !" "What a rip off!"dr Thinking thought.

*"Did you say, rip off ?! Let's try!" He typed the word "rip off" on the keyboard and the message immediately appeared on the video: "The asterisk after each abbreviation indicates that its meaning is not the one declared publicly, but must be looked for in the database of secret acronyms." we are, " dr Suppository shouted." Do you know what this means? "Dr Thinking thought, staring at him with a look that was all a speech." What? "asked dr Suppository "That the abbreviation F.N.P.N. * hides much more; nothing but a new national pension fund! And besides, I always wondered what the accident means that asterisk alongside! Please, try to find out". The search continued spasmodically, until suddenly the words "Secret database data base: set the code you want to know" appeared on the screen. "Hurry, set F.N.P.N" shouted dr Thinking and immediately dr Suppository typed on the keyboard slowly - almost for fear of the answer - the following letters: F.N.P.N. Only a few seconds passed, but it seemed like an eternity and finally the writing F.N.P.N * appeared on the screen: "Fesso ... non ... pago ... niente ..= Cloven = stupid . I. don't ... pay .anything ." And then followed another P.A.P.P. = "Cancellation plan   pension payment "and continued" Since the revenues cannot be*

*increased as it would be an unpopular and counter productive act, all that remains is to reduce the outgoing expenses, most of which are absorbed by pensions. Therefore this plan provides for the gradual elimination of pensionates in an almost ... natural way. The key element was created in our research laboratories, and is marked with the acronym V.A.P. * Exchanging a look, dr Thinking commented: "You understand, this dr Sly (Italian dr Furbetti) ! What a nice plan to eliminate the pensioners! Unfortunate ... Misfortune!" "What do we do now?" Suppositories asked. "You have to understand the plan to the end, especially what this V.A.P. * is. This is the reason for the asterisk, other than a pension increase. The reality is that they intend not to give us anything at all." By now it was getting late, the two friends decided to return the next day and, having put everything in order, they left.*

CHAPTER V.

THE ANTIPENSIONIST VIRUS (V.A.P. *) AND CONTAGIOUS TECHNIQUES

*The next day dr. Thinklng went to work seriously worried and with a lot of anger. At the bar he met dr Suppository, in his own condition, and exclaimed "We must absolutely discover the true meaning of VAP *, other than" Vaccino Going to Pension "! Who knows what it means. We must save m Misfortune, which, for her ....mr Misfortune, it has already been subjected to it! " "Yeah, you're right" - dr Suppository replied - "let's call mr Misfortune immediately and feel how he is, but without telling him anything about this discovery". Dr Thinking called: "Hi, mr Misfortune, how are you?" "Well, why are you asking me this question? You are always well in retirement!" "Not so much". "Thing?" "No nothing, here is dr Suppository with me who greets you" "Warmly reciprocate" replied mr Misfortune..dr Thinking continued "Look, let's meet one of these evenings, okay?" "Yes, alright, bye!" So saying, they hung up. So, reiterated the appointment for the evening, everyone went to their work. In the evening, they managed to enter the offices of the F.N.P.N .. They* *turned on the computer network again. They worked almost all night, until the terrible message appeared on the video: "V.A.P. * = ANTI-PENSION VIRUS: the aspirant retiree is given a dose of immunoglobulin, apparently harmless, but in reality causes death within two months. The contagion techniques are the following: the pensioner, upon submitting the application, must undergo the administration of immunoglobulin to eliminate any occupational diseases. This is to protect the retired citizen free and to safeguard the administration. But, this is not enough, fingerprints are recorded with an infected ink when the first pension is collected. They are also impregnated with the same substance as the payment notice cards, considering that these are always jealously kept by the interested parties. This is also to be able to target those pensioners, who unwittingly managed to avoid contagion by delegating the collection of the pension to another person. The effect is irrelevant for those who have not previously undergone the first dose of V.A.P. *. Little was lacking in such news to dr. Supposed to fail and friend dr Thinking was forced to help him. The dr. Thinking lost his temper and, although bitter, he commented: "More retired so ... you die! There is no way out unless we can find an* *antidote! Anyway, let's go away, we'll talk about it tomorrow!*

"They put everything in order, and went away.

CHAPTER VI

POSTPONEMENT OF THE PENSION APPLICATION

*The following days were very tormented, both for the bad discovery, and for the worries they now had to save their friend mr Misfortune, who had recently undergone the terrible V.A.P. *. What to do for him? Inform him or her of the diabolical P.A.P.P. plan? How to cure it? How to foil the plan? These were the questions that dr Thinking and dr Suppository asked themselves. However, there was no need to waste any more time, the effect of V.A.P. * would not be long in coming. dr. Thinking also had to decide whether or not to submit his pension application. The two friends asked for a few days of leave to discuss and deal with all these problems together. They met at the bar "Il conspiracy "and   dr Thinking said:" The first thing to do is to postpone my pension application, until we find an antidote to the virus, after obviously identifying it. In addition, we absolutely must find a cure for our unfortunate .... mr Misfortune! After so many years of work, of contributions, of uplift, the prize is: "I'm not fucking paid!"   "Of course, if I hadn't read with my own eyes, I wouldn't have believed it. The big problem is mr Misfortune. If we don't find an adequate cure, he will risk* *dying within two months." Do you think he added: "The fact cannot be denounced for various reasons: the first is that we do not yet have a cure, and this would cause panic among pensioners, and then, what evidence can we show? We certainly cannot claim to have searched in the " dr Suppository " archives: "It is not easy to find a cure and an antidote, it takes time to search! ...". And that day also ended. More time passed and the last day came to file the perilous pension application. After all, the only alternative was to prolong the service for another year. That morning the alarm rang as usual, but this time dr Thinking was already awake, indeed that night he hadn't really slept. With his mind he had retraced all the stages of his long career: the years of study and sacrifices at the university, then the internship at the various hospitals, and after, finally, hiring at the current one. Nor had the morning runs taken away from his memory to arrive on time in service despite the intense traffic of the city. He had waited a long time for that day to be able to enjoy his well-deserved rest, after many tribulations. He dreamed of dedicating himself more to the family, in particular to his daughter who had become too young a lady, without him having had the opportunity to realize it. The tribulations were not yet over: the long-awaited and desired day had finally come, and he had nothing else to do but ask to remain on duty again. Oh! Irony of fate! He got up, made very strong coffee and tasted it like never before. Then, thoughtfully, he left, greeting his wife with a simple "hello Ermenziana, see you later!". Arriving at the hospital, his colleagues unaware of the bad news, made him feel sorry. "Your big day has come, think!" said someone, and another: "Finally you will be free!" "Yes, to die!" thought dr Thinking . Nobody could have imagined his decision to remain still in service for attachment ... to life. Great was the internal conflict that dr Thinking experienced that day: on the one hand a great desire to live going towards freedom, on the other that of ... surviving, remaining a game of strength in service.*

He himself diagnosed his torment: "pensive depressive syndrome" S.D.P. Finally he entered the competent office, and in one breath he said: "I do not present any pension application I have decided to remain in service for a year.

Give me the form to fill out!" In the room, great was the silence and wonder, the employees present, amazed, looked at each other, and someone managed, then, to comment: "But as dr.Thinking, but if for at least two years you have done nothing but - let me tell you - to break our soul to know when it could have interrupted "the service, if there was any news, if it had been possible to anticipate the retirement date, etc., and now that you can, give up? "Then the dr Thinking replied:" I realized that only by working, I feel ... alive! "The friend dr Suppository who had accompanied him echoed him:" Me too, when my turn comes, I think I will do the same for love ... of myself! "Having said that, they left. They went to the bar to drink something strong. Here, they met their colleague who, unaware of everything, said to dr Thinking : " Best wishes ,I see you toast to your pension!". "Best wishes to the cabbage, I drink to cheer myself up! So replied, he walked away.

CHAPTER VII

PENSIONAL DEPRESSIVE SYNDROME. S.D.P.

In the following days, we began to read in the newspapers: "It will be pure coincidence, but the reality is that for some time the newly retired within a few months die!" This news was interpreted by most people almost as a curse. And the majority commented: "It will be the .... benefits of the managers of the new pension institution. Do you want to see that they have hired specialized yellers ?!" And again: "Now I understand why the managers of the new institution always wear black, wear an umbrella even when it is not raining and dark glasses even when there is no sun. And so the thousand fantasies increased a real panic. The reactions were the most disparate: some asked for an extension to remain in service, waiting for less times ... blacks, others - although fearing - retired because they thought "better a retired ... dead, than a worker alive. "However, there was a turnaround very soon, that is, the number of those who worked to stay in service increased more and more. All this was attributed to the great fear of dying once put in pension. this confusional   state of mind soon used the same definition created by thinking   for his anguished state: "depressive pension syndrome" with the *abbreviation SDP Others, still, in retirement age, resorted to newly created superstitious talismans, in virtue of which arose a burgeoning market. Among the most famous is the "Pensicorna" (=horns for dr Thinking...) consisting of the classic horns that tighten the pension payment notice card: this was the most requested talisman. The so-called FECAPE or the classic horseshoe magnetizing a plate similar to the model for the pension application made a fine display. In addition, a new superstitious specialization spread: that is, chasing away the iella from pensioners. This specialization was the privilege of those few who took on the title of RI.AI.PE, or retirement anti-ritualists. In essence, these practiced an anti iella ritual, against the managers of the F.N.P.N. * body. By virtue of its particular feature, the fee had to be paid with the first three E 10.00 notes, which were collected on payment of the pension, otherwise the ritual would not have been effective! So it happened that on the day of payment of pensions, outside the post offices a real market of talismans and offers of thaumaturgical services were created: "Buy the Pensicorna, (= horns of dr Thinking ..) buy the FE.CA.PE ...." were the most recurring items from the various street vendors. Nor should we neglect to say that* *when pensioners collected, they paid   great attention to identifying and separating - despite being unaware that they too had been treated with infected liquid - the famous first three E 10.00 banknotes with which to pay for the service offered by RI.ALPE. They were determined to undergo this ritual every month in order to hope to collect the next pension too. The way in which the pensioners withdrew the banknotes was also very particular: both hands closed, like horns! This did not prevent, however, from touching, in addition to the banknotes, also the form - received to compose which had been used the same ink infected by the terrible virus V.A.P. Such was the general scenario. Only dr Thinking e dr Suppository did not adapt to superstitious activity, as they were aware of the anguished truth. Later the two returned to the offices of the F.N.P.N. and they managed to steal other information that proved to be very useful to better define the virus and, therefore, to be able to identify a suitable antidote. It was now time to inform mr Misfortune that he was in danger.When they saw each other again, dr Thinking said: "Dear Misfortune, how do you feel?" "Well since I retired. But why do you always ask me?" "See, we've made a terrible discovery, and it seems right to let you* know." "Are you or I talking, dr Suppository?" "Maybe it's better if you continue, you think!" mr Misfortune intervened: "But, in short, what is it about?" Then dr Thinking explained: "See mr Misfortune, we discovered that ..." and told the terrible truth. At this news mr Misfortune felt bad and repeated: "Oh! Unfortunate me!" "Come on, don't go overboard –dr Thinking continued: we will certainly find a solution. We must never lose hope, sweet bearer of good news" dr Thinking - please - I am thinking about my serious situation and you are babbling with hope! "At this point intervened dr Suppository :" Do not worry. A first antiviral drug will soon be ready to block the devastating effect of VAP * If we weren't sure, we certainly wouldn't have revealed anything to you! "mr Misfortune calmed down and asked:" Really true, are you sure you don't tell me nonsense? "" In a few days, I assure you that the first doctor will be ready "confirmed dr Thinking ". Well! at this point my talismans are no longer needed! "and so saying he threw them all away. Do you think he asked:" Where are the banknotes you collected first? "." Which? Which ones to pay the RI.AI.PE.? "asked mr Misfortune." Yes. "" Here they are. "" So, since you no longer need them – dr Thinking continued - I'll take *them, because they can be of great help in my research. Now let's go eat something. "But, you have absolutely no respect for anything," dr Suppository intervened. "Come on, let's not dramatize" you think "I'm a virologist, you're a pharmacologist, so certainly with the commitment of both, soon there will be the right medicine to cure this VAP or whatever the hell it is called. Then we'll see how to proceed to Now, I repeat, let's go eat something, we have to be strong, otherwise how can we work to find the right medicine ?! ". "Oh! ... I understand, let's go!" mr Misfortune replied, So, calm and confident they went to the nearby restaurant.*

CHAPTER VIII

THE PILL ATTEND 7 and 1/2 AND THE LIQUID LIQUID PENSIONS

After several attempts dr. Thinking with the aid of electron microscopy identified the killer virus present on the banknotes and in close collaboration with dr. Suppositories - after numerous laboratory tests - came to the discovery of a first effective drug on the viral replication of V.A.P., thus slowing down its effects Successful in their intent, they immediately telephoned their friend mr Misfortune: "We have good news to give you: we have a first healing drug! We are waiting for you at the 'Il Complotto' bar"(= Conspiracy bar). Very punctual they were at the bar dr Thinking , dr Suppository and poor Dr Misfortune, who immediately asked anxiously: "What is it about?". We have the medicine that extends ... the pension. It is a pack of four tablets called ATTEND 7 and 1/2, because each one extends the life of the pensioner by seven and a half days, for a total of thirty days, therefore it allows to collect another whole pension " "Well! It's not much, but it's already a first result, isn't it?" said dr Thinking to encourage his friend mr Misfortune. Then he added: "I'm sure that dr. Suppository, who will never miss my collaboration, will find the final drug. "" Then I just have to take these tablets. Do you have them with you? " mr Misfortune asked." No, wait, there's another thing you need to know, "she continued." What? "" There are some unpleasant side effects to consider! "." What do you mean, explain yourself better! "."Listen to me carefully: the first tablet should be taken within twenty minutes from the collection of the next pension, and this is not a problem, but the real one is the side effects to endure. And, being a new drug, I know it involves ... strong abdominal pain, but I can't know what intensity they are ". "And can't pain be alleviated in any way?" mr Misfortune replied. "Well! There would be a way! Since the pains depend on the lot of air that forms inside the intestine, you should strive to release it all and the pain will cease. Then you feel like taking ATTEND 7 and 1 /2?" (= WAIT 7 AND ½)) mr Misfortune was a bit perplexed, then remarked: "Yes, but as you do, in a Post Office with so many people present it doesn't seem decent to me. However, being there twenty minutes, we will try to get away in the shortest possible time". The friend Thoughts to dispel worries and in still a little seriousness, he remembered and recited the poetry of an anonymous but great poet: "Vulgar is *considered the fart, but if the pain is great and the effect is beneficial , thunder your ass too, and blessed! ". "And don't forget - added dr. Thinking - our great father Dante:" And he had trumpet of which "Inf. Canto ..verso   x (=hellish song towards x .).? So the conversation left the tragic tone with a beautiful smile of the three friends! Reassured mr Misfortune, he made a new appointment directly at the Post Office, when he would go to collect the pension. And that day, dr mr mr mr mr Misfortune lined up at the post office, accompanied by dr Thinking , waiting for his shift. dr Suppository was waiting in the car, parked right in front of the Post Office with an ATTEND 7 and 1/2 tablet, ready for use and with a nice glass of water. When his turn came, collected his pension and ran out with dr Thinking towards the car; they entered, sat down and with a sip of water mr Misfortune swallowed the now famous tablet. Then followed a great silence, waiting ... for the side effects, which were not long in making themselves felt: excruciating pain for the unfortunate one .... mr Misfortune, who began to twist on himself and to massage his unfortunate abdomen. Then the dr. Supposed: "Strive, strive, remember our advice". The dr. Thinking echoed, and while such encouragement followed mr*

Misfortune emitted ... and ... it seemed a roar, but the pain eased .In that while a funeral procession unfolded in respectful silence, and suddenly mr Misfortune he freed for the second time. But ... if no external effect had occurred before, now the repetition caused amazement, marvels and, for those who understood anger and disgust. Meanwhile, the pains returned more violent than ever and to avoid further external effects, dr. Supposed while trying to get away from the traffic, he shouted "Hold yourself back, let's get out of here, soon" And you thought he was exhorting in the same way. ... By now it was too late to hide and, seeing them indicated by finger from the present, they increased the speed. A diligent vigilant, however, managed to read the plaque, reserving the right to verify if this noise was part of the crime of "disturbing the ... public peace" and then subjecting them to a regular fine. In any case, the administration of the first dose of medicine was earlier: there was now another month to be able to search for a more potent drug. When the effect of the last tablet of ATTEND 7 and 1/2 was almost expiring, dr Suppository telephoned dr Thinking: "I have news to give you: I found another drug" "Well !, compliments, let's meet tonight at the usual bar with mr Misfortune too, and we'll talk about it," said dr Thinking. La evening everyone was punctual, as usual. "Finally I took a step forward" began the suppositories "I found a new drug that lengthens ... the pension of two others months ". "What is it about?" mr Misfortune asked anxiously once more. Supposed he explained: "It is a liquid, which I have signed L.L.P., or liquidated pension liquid, which is administered with an enema!" "Tell me what the side effects are now, don't keep me anxious," said mr Misfortune. "Yes, actually, there are some drawbacks, small, but there is: you will feel the need to go to the bathroom urgently," dr Suppository explained. Then mr Misfortune commented: "Well! It's not a big problem ..." "I don't know, however, remember that the enema must be practiced within twenty minutes from the collection of the next pension mr Misfortune, addressed to dr Thinking , asked:" What do you think ... Think? ... "What do you want me to tell you! If the liquid brings money, you can go in abundantly and do not complain. On the other hand, if you interrupt, you will have extended your life by only a month!" "You're right. Okay, we'll see you at the post office later this month." So saying, they said goodbye. Then, all three met very punctually. The dr.Tthinking , mr Misfortune was in line at the counter in the post office, while dr. Suppository was ready outside, in the car. As soon as mr Misfortune got his pension, he hurriedly headed for the car and sat down next to dr Suppository while dr Thinking drove. The execution took place! A profound silence followed! Pending the side effect, it was decided to find a secluded and ... green place, perhaps in order to be protected from prying eyes. mr Misfortune mr Misfortun relaxed and began to say: "I feel   really good, I don't feel ... mima you couldn't finish the sentence, that a strange gurgling announced an urgent need to go to the bathroom!" Quick Think, quick! "Think The violations of the highway code were not late and soon a police patrol - with sirens explained - began to chase them. Meanwhile, Misfortune: "Run, be quick, please, I can't take it anymore! ... but dr Suppository ordered: "No, stop, there is the police chasing us". The unfortunate dr Thinking no longer knew what to do. Meanwhile, a truck cut across the road and dr Thinking hit him. The policemen, convinced that they were facing real criminals, got out of the car with weapons in hand, and ordered: "Hands up and come out!".   Poor mr Misfortune went out first, but only because of his urgent need, and he *didn't stop ... he had much more to think about! The policemen fired a few shots into the air for intimidation. This did nothing but accelerate ... the poor man's already urgent need, which ... suddenly came to the point! The conclusion - then - was to meet at the police headquarters, where it was not easy for both doctors to justify their positions, without of course telling the complete truth. They claimed that their friend mr Misfortune had felt bad. However mr Misfortune managed to earn two months of retirement, waiting for a better drug to definitively eradicate the terrible V.A.P. **

CHAPTER IX

THE A.V.A.P SUPPOSITIONS AND THE ALLELUIA SUPPOSTONE

A few weeks passed. Before the effect of the last cure ended, dr. Thinking - while resting on the sofa meditating on the agonizing "go or not retire" problem - he jumped at the sudden ringing of the phone: "Hi, dr Thinking , I have developed a new drug much more effective, and anyway I think to be one step away from the final one ". "Finally - answered dr Thinking breathing a sigh of relief - but, given the previous experiences, what are the side effects, this time?". "Let's meet with mr Misfortune two hours at the usual bar and we'll talk about it. Hello." Very punctual they met and Dr Misfortune: "Tell me immediately what effects ..." "Do not be stupid interrupted. Think - the important thing is to find a final cure, which will make you heal completely, whatever the side effect "..mr Misfortune .resigned himself. dr Suppository explained: "This is the supposed A.V.A.P., or anti-anti-tension virus. It, applied within ten minutes of collecting the next pension, extends it for another two months" "The effects, please?" "Misfortune, don't worry, this time they are mild: a little ... smelly intestinal gases originate". "Well! It doesn't seem a big inconvenience to me. Do you think ... what do you think?" "The clear and pure air is everywhere, however and always, ready to depart even every little trace in the evaporation of any pleasant or not pleasant smell". dr Thinking said. "Okay, once again you convinced me" was mr Misfortune's reply. They met at the usual post office. On the day of collection they met and everyone was in his place: Thinking in line with Dr Misfortune; Supposed in the car. As for the side effects, dr. they decided to take their friend to the open countryside to make them more comfortable and to leave the car windows open, for the sake of themselves. As soon as he retired, mr Misfortune ran away to the car, followed by dr Thinking . Supposed to drive, already with the engine running - as soon as mr Misfortune and dr Thinking entered - he started rocket.mr Misfortune applied the supposed A.V.A.P. A great silence followed, pending the now famous side effects, of which dr Suppository himself ignored the entity, for which he had proceeded to buy some deodorants. The side effect did not take long: an unbreathable gas spread in the car so quickly and suddenly that I only gave Time to say: "I'm starting to feel ... but ... leee" and passed out. The car stopped suddenly without a driver, while it was going at high speed. You think, while trying to use the deodorant and to hold on to the internal supports, he shouted: "Try to brake, brake ...". The car, in no time, swabbed a running bus violently. Obviously the driver and several people immediately got out and surrounded the car. Meanwhile the poisonous vapors continued slowly but surely to spread. Suddenly someone shouted, "There is a gas leak!" and a general "run, run" began. Some good people evidently phoned 113 and in a short time the firefighters and some ambulances arrived. The three were taken to hospital and subjected to others, with a detoxifying treatment. In spite of everything, this time too they had earned two months' penance. Now greater was the hope of reaching the final act for Dr Misfortune. One day dr Thinking telephoned dr Suppository: "Dear friend, I appreciate your goodwill, but if to retire, you must undergo your tortures, I give up. I prefer to remain in service until the end of my days!". " "Don't worry, I just have to perfect the last drug. As soon as it's ready, I'll call you": "No, I don't worry, but you scare me."

"Hi". After a few weeks, now nearing the end of the effect of the last cure, dr Thinking received yet another call in the middle of the night from dr Suppository this time very happy: "I am here, I finally found the drug for the total inactivation of the _lethal V.A.P virus." You immediately think asked: "The side effects, tell me immediately what they are, otherwise I will not come to the appointment!" "Don't worry, there are none of a clinical nature, but healing is assured. Do you understand ?, it heals completely." "And, alright, see you later with Dr Misfortune!" "See you later, bye". When they met, mr Misfortune claimed he preferred death, to unacceptable effects. And Suppository: "But dear, this medicine has the power to inactivate the virus and make you recover permanently" "Let me explain - dr Suppository continued, showing a box - you see, here is your salvation. It is a simple suppository, called by me ALLELUIA, to indicate the joy of healing". "The effects, I want to know the side effects!" mr Misfortune insisted. "There are no clinical side effects. dr Suppository applied within five minutes of collecting the next pension is enough, and it is done. The side effects, improperly said, in this case, are intrinsically linked to the characteristics of the suppository itself." "What do you

mean ? "mr Misfortune asked. "I mean that ..." and opening the box, he showed a huge suppository of about six hundred meters "Nooo!" mr Misfortune exclaimed. At this point, dr. Think and, as always, managed to calm and convince at the same time his unfortunate friend. So, once again reiterated the same appointment, they say goodbye. After meeting ,dr Thinking queued up with mr Misfortune to collect the pension, while dr Suppository waited outside by the car. This time they had decided that mr Misfortune would apply the medicine alone, in the car conveniently placed in a somewhat secluded place. The supposed ALLELUIA was showing off on the dashboard of the car! In the meantime, do you think continued to encourage mr Misfortune: "Come on, think this is the last time, you have to apply the suppository at any cost, after you will be completely cured. We will follow you immediately ... in retirement ". Finally, it was the turn of mr Misfortune to collect the pension, then running towards the car. Alone ... he went in and ... got busy. For a while, no signal came from inside the car, when suddenly, "ALLELUIA ... ah! ... ah! ..." was heard and it was not clear if it was cries of joy to be healed or ... of pain, for the size of the suppository. Both dr. they were happy with the recovery, but were shocked by the reaction of mr Misfortune.. Timidly they opened the car door and saw poor mr Misfortune who, he repeated: "I am cured but oh! What pain .... what pain! ...". The passers by, observing, commented: "But the unfortunate one will have gone mad! .._ mr Misfortune was then bedridden for a few days for the necessary treatment, but he was delighted to finally be able to receive the pension for the rest of the In the meantime the two doctors reflected and you think: "Dear Suppository, this ... you put it on you! If this is the only way to secure a lifetime pension, I prefer to remain on duty until the end of mine days! "And Suppositories:" Well! in fact, not even for me, okay, we need to find a less traumatic way of administering the vaccine ". So, they said goodbye, happy to have saved their friend, but a little doubtful of being able to save themselves ... from the terrible supposed ALLELUIA.

CHAPTER X

THE VA.VA. ANTIPENSIONISTIC ANTIVIRUS VACCINE TIE

In the following days, there was intense work by dr. Suppository to identify a more suitable route of administration of the vaccine. The fear of the supposed ALLELUIA made him work day and night. Often he also consulted with df Thinking on the phone. By now the hopes were fading as the next deadline for being able to present the pension application by dr. Thinking .Ma one evening came to dr Thinking the long-awaited and awaited phone call: "You can finally retire! And soon after I will come too: I have found the final solution". Dr Thinking was puzzled for a moment, then asked: "What about the side effects ?!" "Do not worry, this time they are also beneficial. I assure you of this, have confidence and you will see ..." he said with a reassuring tone. "You won me over, let's meet tomorrow morning with mr Misfortune at the hospital bar". The next day, when they met, dr Suppository appeared satisfied and happy and immediately said: "Gene therapy: the new frontier of medicine. Let me explain right away. I consulted a friend of mine professor at the University of Bethesda, who uses this therapy with genes suitably "built" in a molecular biology laboratory. These genes are of a heterogeneous substance of a protein nature which, when penetrated into the organism, determines the production of antibodies ". The V.A.VA.TIÈ vaccine must be administered within ten minutes from the time that the pension application will be submitted. You will have to inject with your right arm outstretched, while your left hand, with your arm bent, supports it at the internal height of your elbow. The right hand is held closed. The side effects are harmless, indeed good luck and you will discover them at the moment. I assure you that this time they are really pleasant for us.   "" I have to trust, asked dr Thinking   since will I be the next sucking guinea pig? "" Trust me, "replied dr Suppository." But, explain one last thing, I understand the initials VAVA, but TIÈ what does it indicate in the acronym? "" Precisely this you will know at the same time that it will be injected you, "concluded Suppositories." Is there anything else I need to know? "she continued." Yes, you must know that the we call will be made upon collection of the first thirteenth pension. This I called T.VA.VA, in which T

indicates exactly thirteenth. "At the end, dr Thinking said:"
Then I just have to retire, exactly in eight days. To you my
praise and my 'heartfelt thanks'. "

CHAPTER XI

THE DR. THINK GOES IN BOARD

The evening before the long-awaited day finally came. During the night dr Thinking was unable to sleep, for the immense joy. He daydreamed of everything he could have done: sleeping in the morning so far uncontrolled, going out for long walks during the beautiful days, or reading his beloved books. The following morning he got up cheerfully and the alarm did not ring this time. He made himself a good cup of coffee, said goodbye to his wife and left. Arriving at the office, he found his friends dr Suppository and mr Misfortune who had organized everything to inject the VA.VA.TIÈ vaccine ten minutes after submitting the application. The car, as usual, was parked right outside the hospital, with the engine running and mr Misfortune driving it: for the first time, he was not a guinea pig. Accompanied by his colleague, dr Thinking _ presented the question and hurriedly left with him. They found the elevator busy, then running down the stairs and then towards the car. They got into the car and at great speed mr Misfortune headed for the laboratory located in the large square nearby, on the fourth *floor, right in front of the offices of the F.N.P.N. * body. All three rushed into the laboratory; the dr. _Thinking _ raised his shirt sleeves and as dr Suppository had explained, he positioned his right arm outstretched, with his fist closed, while the hand of his left arm bent, supported him at the height of the elbow bend. The dr. Suppository injected the vaccine into his left forearm ... while dr Thinking with his imagination, he already saw himself as a happy pensioner. At this point the side effects occurred, so that the right arm and clenched fist stiffened, the left hand clenched stronger; and ... all three in chorus, they repeated in rapid succession: "TIÈ. TTÈ. TIÈ, all three retired". All of this happened with the gaze turned to the offices of the famous institution F.N.P.N. * located right in front of it. Dr Thinking commented: "Now I understand what the abbreviation ITE indicates, of the VA.VA.TIÈ vaccine". Then they went to the bar to toast happy for the very successful operation. In December dr Thinking also managed to collect the thirteenth, and the T.VA.VA. recall, or thirteenth anti-pension virus vaccine, was also injected. Following the dr. Furbetti president of the institution and all his collaborators were sentenced following the complaint lodged by the doctors Thinking   and dr*

Suppository and by dr Misfortune. So the dr. Do you think, he could finally become a gentleman do you think ... honored, followed by dr. Suppository, who was delighted that his name remained forever in the international pharmacopoeia. They lived retired and happy for a long time and not only them, but also their spouses who, due to the reversibility, were able to enjoy, in the face of all present and future reformers, the pension system.

* * * *

The End

www.ingramcontent.com/pod-product-compliance
Lightning Source LLC
Chambersburg PA
CBHW020513160726
47991CB00007B/2937